The Fifty-Dollar Eggs

by

Kevin D. Finson

(2nd Edition)

© by Finson, 2024. All rights reserved. No part of this publication may be reproduced or used in any form or by any means, electronic or mechanical, including photocopying, recording, or by any information storage and retrieval system, without the express written permission from the copyright owner. For information regarding permission, write to: **kevindfinsonauthor@gmail.com** .

ISBN: 979-8-9917564-8-8
Imprint: Independently Published

Dedicated to my parents and family who taught me how to give of ourselves to others, even in difficult times.

One of the true gems of life is when someone gives of themselves to help others. It is especially true when that giving arises on the spur of the moment in unplanned ways. This is a story of a young man's search for special gifts for his family that would go beyond just the basic necessities, and found a much larger treasure in sharing what he found with strangers who were in need. What he found in that second-hand store that day would find a place in his heart and would bring him more deeply into a life lived well.

The Fifty-Dollar Eggs

There are times in life when trying to live well is easy, and there are times when it is difficult. And what defines "living life well" can mean different things to different people. For some, living well means accumulating wealth -- such as money and luxuries. For others, it means living in ways that provide for basic yet comfortable necessities. It can also mean living in ways that are wholesome, including kindness and a willingness to help others in their times of need, even when one's own resources are not very plentiful.

Garnet was a young man who was seeking to live life well. He had no pretense of becoming wealthy in terms of money or luxuries. That was not an opportunity people of his social status were afforded in the early 1900s. Of course, many might dream of such things, but the reality was they would not be able to accomplish it. Instead, they tended to settle into a life where they could provide for themselves adequate shelter, sufficient but not bountiful food, and some minimal comforts just slightly above what were considered the bare necessities. When those small things arrived, they were treasured. People worked very hard for what they had, and placed a high value on doing work well and doing it honestly.

Another trait of people in Garnet's social level was an attitude of taking care of each other. Although nobody had an overabundance of resources, they would still manage to somehow draw from them to rally and help others who were in need. Even a few cents here or there could make a big difference to someone, as might an additional loaf of home-baked bread, some fruit or vegetables from a garden, or some hand-stitched repairs on a worn-out garment. Garnet had learned those kinds of lessons about life from his parents. And it was through applying those lessons to his living that Garnet found happiness and satisfaction with life. In fact, most people in Garnet's family and neighborhood were happy and content. They may not have always been comfortable or without worry, but they were happy and content. In a way, such things brought peace to them. Those were the true gems of life. Those were the gems of living life well.

In what was an unusual circumstance, Garnet was given an opportunity to do some extra work at his job. Although the regular work hours already made for long days, Garnet was happy with the chance to do some extra work and earn a few more dollars. The extra cash would allow him to do some special things for his family -- to perhaps secure some gifts that would lift a little bit of their lives just above the bare necessities. Each had given up much over time to make sure others had what they needed. To Garnet, that was incentive to do something unexpected and special for them.

The extra work would be hard, but Garnet believed it would be worth it. He knew the over-time work would not last very long, but he wanted to take advantage of it as long as it was available to him. There would be some sacrifices to be made in order to put in that extra time at his job. He would have less time with his family, less time with his friends, and -- of course -- less time to rest. But in the end, Garnet had managed to save fifty dollars from that extra work. It was a phenomenal amount considering the financial situations of most families at that time in his part of town when most only earned about eight hundred dollars in a year.

As one of his rare days off work neared, Garnet began considering his task of searching the shops in town for the perfect gifts for his family. Although fifty dollars was a lot of money to him, it wouldn't carry too far in some stores. The merchandise in them was too luxurious and much too expensive. And, most of it would not really be of much use to his family. What he had to find were things that could be helpful and useful. They had to be practical in some way. They had to be things that would endure. They had to be like gems in their lives, things that would be treasured. He decided the best places to look would be in the smaller shops dotting the narrower streets and alleys extending beyond the main avenues. When his day off arrived, Garnet arose early and set off for the small shops.

Strolling along the sidewalks, Garnet would peer into the windows of the shops he passed. Most of the time, he didn't see anything through the windows that enticed him to go inside. Once in a while, something caught his eye and he would go into a shop and investigate what they had for sale. Nothing seemed to suit his wants, however, so he continued strolling along the sidewalks hoping to come across some gems in one of the shops.

Just as he was about to give up for the day, he came to an old building off to the side of the street almost in the alley. The building had seen better days. Its brickwork was intricate and of the kind done decades earlier. The mortar between the bricks was in need of some repair. The wood trim around the windows was in need of repainting, as was the doorframe. The door was a double one with wood panels on the lower half that were in need of patching and painting. Frosted glass panels graced its upper half and had traces of long-worn-off lettering on them that once identified the shop.

Garnet couldn't really see much of anything through the windows, but something in the back of his mind was pushing him to go in. So, Garnet pushed the door open, and its quiet squeak announced his entry. It opened much easier than he expected from the sound it made. His first steps inside were met with the creaking of old wood floorboards.

The shop was not like the typical ones farther back along the street. Those shops tended to specialize in single kinds of items, such as clothing or jewelry or kitchenware. But this shop was more eclectic. It was like a flea market or second-hand store filled with a hodge-podge of many different kinds of things. Garnet had a feeling some treasures could be found hiding somewhere amongst the shelves in the shop. The sunlight from behind him flooded in and illuminated the floor as if marking out for him a path to follow into the depths of the shop.

The old wooden floor creaked with each step Garnet took. It was as if the floor was announcing his route. The shop was full of all sorts of things. None of it was new. It was obviously old stuff, but from what Garnet could see it was in good condition. It was also obvious each item had been caringly put in its place on the shelves. Nothing was jumbled or in disarray. It seemed an odd juxtaposition of old things put carefully into an arrangement like new things in the other shops.

Garnet began to think about what each member of his family would enjoy as a gift. He first thought of his nephew. His nephew liked books. He was just eight years old, but already had a library of several books in his bedroom. Garnet knew most of the books his nephew had in the collection, so he wanted to find something that would be different. Perhaps a classic? He soon found himself in front of a shelf of books. Taking one off the shelf, he read the title and opened the book and flipped gently through its pages. He returned the book and selected another one.

Garnet lost track of how long he had been in front of the shelf and how many books he thumbed through, but he finally came across one he thought his nephew would like. It was entitled, *The Wolflings*. A small paper tag was attached to the book: the price tag. Only fifteen cents -- a very reasonable cost. Its cover showed it had been well-loved, yet it was not tattered or dirty.

Garnet pursed his lips and opened the book. The story was one of deep friendships. It was about a young boy who lived in the country. He was an only child and evidently lonely. One day, his father brought the boy a puppy. The boy and puppy bonded quickly and were inseparable. Garnet knew his nephew liked dogs, but didn't have one. The family couldn't afford to support a pet. So, this book might be perfect for him.

Garnet found himself unable to turn his eyes away from the book and continued reading. The boy would take his puppy and wander all around their farm. One day, the two found themselves deep in the woods in the back acres of the farm. The boy rarely went there. His father had not encouraged him going there, but had not discouraged him outright from doing so.

Suddenly, the boy and the puppy walked out into a glen, or a meadow, surrounded by trees of the woods. There was plenty of space in the meadow to run and jump, to roll in the grass, and to let someone feel totally free. It was a place the boy and puppy would return to over and over again. It was a special place for them, one that was almost like a secret hideaway.

On one visit, they heard a rustling sound amongst the trees. It was a pack of wolves. They were young wolves, at least six of them. The boy and puppy were startled, and at first fearful of what the wolves might do. Suddenly, the puppy jumped and ran toward the wolves. The boy wasn't sure if the puppy was charging at the wolves to protect him. And the wolves bounded toward the boy and puppy. As it turned out, the young wolves wanted to play. They, the boy and puppy jumped around the meadow together and had the most wonderful time! It was such a wonderful and exhilarating time that the boy, puppy, and wolves returned there year after year. Those rendezvous continued as the boy grew into a young man and the puppy into a devoted dog. The young man protected the wolves and the wolves protected the young man and dog. Garnet thought this would be exactly the kind of story his nephew would enjoy and read over and over again. So, he tucked the book under his arm and then turned to move further into the old shop.

    Garnet next found himself in a section of the shop containing items related to music. His mother was very fond of music, and had instilled in him a deep respect for it. She had a particular fondness for classical music. Garnet's mother had inherited an old violin from her grandmother. It was not anything one might consider special like a Stradivarius, but it was nevertheless treasured and cared for with much love. It was an heirloom. No one seemed to know how his grandmother had come to possess the violin. It was not exactly a carefully-guarded secret, but his grandmother never spoke about it. It was just information no one seemed to know. It was one of those mysterious family secrets that sometimes exist in a family.

    His mother had learned to play the instrument, and mostly reserved her playing to herself or family. She did not play professionally, although Garnet thought she could have done so. The sounds she enticed from

the violin were the sweetest of melodies. But there was just no time for her to be away from her work supporting the family and maintaining the household for her to be away practicing and performing.

    Garnet had been blessed his mother taught him the basics of playing that violin. He learned as she had learned -- mostly by ear. Rarely did they have access to sheet music. If they had a piece, it was borrowed for only a short time from a teacher or friend. They could not afford to purchase any of their own. But when they had some, they would hone their note-reading skills. Garnet would sometimes try to copy some on small scraps of paper using a pencil that always seemed exceedingly dull. He was certain his mother would be pleased with receiving a copy of classical sheet music.

    On the shelf before him was a stack of it. Most was written for piano, but there were some for other instruments. After sifting through the stack, Garnet found several that were specifically composed for violin. He studied each carefully, trying to find one that was classical in genre. Soon, he found several. Each had a paper price tag attached to it. The prices were scribbled in pencil, and all were the same: fifteen cents per piece. Garnet thought that a very reasonable price, and gathered all the classical music sheets, tucking them between the covers of the book he selected for his nephew so the sheets would not get bent or folded. So far, Garnet was pleased with the gems he was finding for his family in that old shop.

As Garnet turned, he spotted some other music items on the shelving behind him. The first thing that caught his eye was an old record player. It was actually a gramophone. It was the kind that had a crank on its side that had to be turned in order to wind the spring inside to make the turntable go around. The bell on the top seemed to be in exceptionally good condition. Garnet looked closely at the needle, and found it intact. He grasped the handle of the crank and gave it a slight turn. It seemed stiff enough, but not too much so. That indicated the spring inside was intact and not wound too tight or broken.

Garnet thought the gramophone would be the perfect gift for his father. His father would listen to music whenever he had a chance. Garnet remembered how his father would sit back in his stuffed chair, eye closed, smiling as he'd listen to his mother playing her violin.

As with his mother, Garnet's father especially liked classical music. His father would relish the times when he was invited to a neighbor's house to sit and listen to their record player. It seemed to bring some peace to his father after long hard days of work or when he hit a rough patch in life. Garnet thought it would be ideal for his father to have his own gramophone so he could listen to it whenever he wanted. And the price tagged to it was fifteen dollars. Garnet pursed his lips and gave a slight nod of his head as if to tell the old music box he approved.

The gramophone was large enough that carrying it along with the book and sheet music would be awkward. So, Garnet placed the book and sheet music on the shelf next to the gramophone and lifted the record player. It was a little heavier than Garnet had anticipated, causing him to let out a soft groan.

He turned and walked toward the shop counter and set it down where there was space. The counter was

made of large planks of rough-hewn wood that had been smoothed over many years from an untold number of people rubbing their arms and hands across it. The wood had been polished smooth in that way.

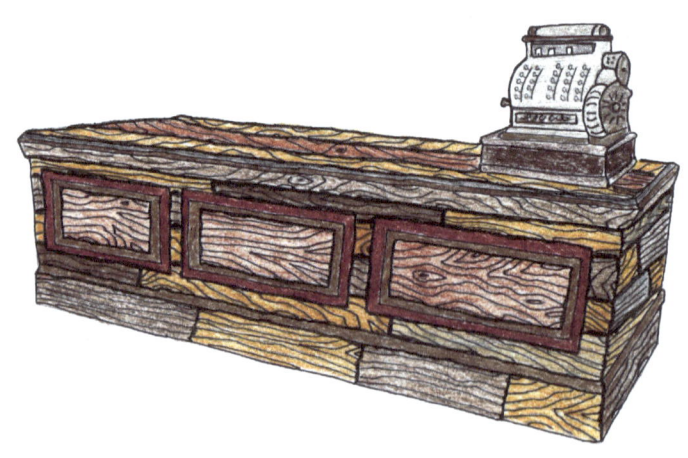

The shopkeeper stood behind the counter, and smiled as he watched Garnet maneuver the gramophone into its place. "You've got a good eye!" said the shopkeeper.

"More like a good ear, I hope." replied Garnet.

"That music box you have there is really something. What kind of music do you like best?" asked the shopkeeper.

Garnet stammered slightly, "Oh, different kinds. Probably classical the most, I guess. But this isn't for me. It's for my father." He patted the gramophone with the palm of his hand.

"Oh, I see." answered the shopkeeper. "Does your father have records to play on it?"

Garnet stood upright with a startled look in his eyes. "No, he doesn't!"

The shopkeeper smiled. "Perhaps you should think about getting some? There's a stack of them back on the shelf next to where that music box was."

Garnet turned to look back toward the music section of the shop. He sighed. "Yes, yes. A good idea! Thanks!"

With that, Garnet left the gramophone on the counter and strolled back to the music shelves. There, he found a small stack of old records, just as the shopkeeper had told him. They were the typical kind of records of that time -- thick black ones, made of shellac. Most were held inside thick paper covers or sleeves that had turned brown over the years.

Garnet carefully shuffled through the stack of records, selecting one and reading its label, and then

slid the record out of its sleeve so he could examine its condition. He held it up so the light would reflect off its surface so he could see if it had scratches across it. The needle of the gramophone would skip on those scratches and not play well. The record was almost pristine and without blemish. Garnet carefully re-inserted it into its sleeve and repeated a similar examination of each of the other records. To his surprise, each passed his inspection.

Next, Garnet looked at the labels on each of the records. The labels were certainly old. Some had a purplish-color with gold print on them. Despite their age, one could still clearly read what the music was. Near the bottom of the stack, Garnet discovered one record labeled *The Emperor's Waltz* and another labeled *The Water Music*. There was also the *Blue Danube Waltz*, the *Royal Fireworks, A Little Night Music, Serenade for Strings, The Sleeping Beauty Waltz, and Canon in D*. Garnet was sure his father would like any of them. He looked at the price tag that had laid on the top of the stack. It indicated each record was priced at twenty-five cents. Garnet at first thought the price a bit high, but then realized there were usually two records in each sleeve, not just one. So, it was more of a bargain than at first appearance. The group of them would make for a wonderful collection for his father. Garnet picked up his eight selections, plus the book and sheet music, and returned to the shop counter where he laid them next to the gramophone.

The shopkeeper tapped each with the tip of his index finger. "Very nice choices! Very nice! Will that be all for today?" He raised one eyebrow.

Garnet started to say, "Yes," but stopped. "Yes . . ., er, no! I still need to find something for my brother! I'll be right back!" He quickly turned from the counter and stepped back amongst the towering shelves, almost tripping over his own foot. His eyes wandered back and forth as he pondered what his brother might like. He was thinking so deeply he really didn't see where he was going, and startled himself when bumping into a shelf containing some toys. Garnet wasn't sure his brother would want a toy. He did seem to like collecting things that were shiny, like crystals of minerals, beads, and glass items. Some of his brother's most favorite things were glass. His brother particularly liked the way they glistened and glowed when he held them up to the sunlight.

Garnet rubbed his chin and stepped to his right to leave the toy section of the shop. But before he took a second step, he caught sight of some glistening glimmering shiny things just an arm's length away, resting near the front edge of one of the shelves. But it was not just one thing. It was a dozen. It was a set of glass marbles.

A ray of sunlight peeked through a spot on the window and was focused precisely on the marbles. Garnet could tell they were made of very old glass due to the tiny bubbles trapped within them. He picked one up and held it up to his eye so the sunlight shining through the shop's window would pass through it. The tiny orb glistened and glowed, just like Garnet's brother would like. Garnet carefully examined each of the twelve marbles and marveled at the variety of colors and swirls that were held within them. Next to the marbles was a small leather satchel, just the right size to hold the whole bunch. The price tag showed three cents each. Garnet could hardly pass up such a bargain! The set of marbles and their pouch soon joined Garnet's other gems on the shop counter.

Looking over his stash, Garnet stepped back a step from the counter, his hands on his hips. He glanced up at the shopkeeper, and for the first time really made a close observation of the man. The shopkeeper was old, or more appropriately grandfatherly, in appearance. He had grey eyebrows that seemed to hold up the front of his unruly hair. His mustache matched his eyebrows in a funny sort of way. There was an odd depth to his eyes, which had a joyful gleam in them that was hard to look away from. Old faded pants were held up by suspenders that wrapped up and over the shoulders of a checkered shirt whose sides had come untucked from the pants. Garnet wasn't sure of the colors. Maybe blue, perhaps green, or they might have been a brown. Garnet's attention was mostly fixed on the shopkeeper's eyes. Funny, but he wasn't even sure about the color of the shopkeeper's eyes.

The shopkeeper then asked, "Are there any other treasures you need to find?" His voice was smooth and calming -- and almost playful. It had a kind and inviting tone to it -- a tone that would draw a listener in deeper and deeper with each word spoken. It was a peaceful voice. Garnet suddenly found himself quieting and feeling more peaceful than he had for quite some time.

"Yes, I think I've found just the right things!" replied Garnet with a smile.

"That's good," said the shopkeeper. "It is always good when you can find good matches for the folks you're shopping for. Anything for yourself?"

"Me? For me?" Garnet mumbled. He shook his head a little from side to side as if to clear his head. "I hadn't thought about anything for myself. I guess it would be nice to have a trinket or two -- nothing big, of course. Just something to make me smile a little more each day."

"May I suggest you browse the back area of the shop?" the shopkeeper said.

"The back?" murmured Garnet. "Yes, yes, the back. I didn't get back there. I'd best take a look in the back!"

At first glance from the counter, the back of the shop looked like a dungeon. But as Garnet walked toward it, he found it just as inviting as the front of the shop. Perhaps it was just the way the light filtered through the back windows. It wasn't quite as bright as the front part of the shop, but there was ample light.

Garnet strolled amongst the shelving, glancing one way and then the other as he walked. He had not really thought about what he might buy for himself. He really didn't think he needed anything in particular. Perhaps it was a time to get something a little less than practical, maybe something whimsical? Garnet puzzled about it for a while. He was thinking more than looking as he strolled, and wasn't paying much attention to the items he was passing on the shelving.

A flash of light startled Garnet and aroused him from his thoughts. It was a beam of sunlight poking through the glass panes of a skylight overhead. The beam seemed to illuminate a single spot on one shelf. The old wooden floorboards creaked as Garnet stepped toward the it. Highlighted in the sun, Garnet saw two alabaster eggs. Italian alabaster eggs. They were not large -- just the size of chicken eggs.

But their appearance almost had a hypnotic effect. Each egg had been hand-carved, polished, and dyed. Their surfaces reflected light almost like a mirror while at the same time seeming to draw light deep into them in a way that made them glow.

Garnet was almost entranced with the eggs. Colored veins wiggled their way through the alabaster as if trying to make a pattern out of something chaotic. Yet out of that chaos arose something beautifully defined and shaped, something pleasing to the eye and soothing to the touch. These were certainly things Garnet would cherish, and things that would constantly remind him of the peacefulness he felt in that old shop. On the price tag was scrawled "three dollars". Garnet thought it a low price for something so nice. So, he picked up the two alabaster eggs and walked back to the shop counter cradling them in his hands.

The shopkeeper gave Garnet a broad smile. "I see you've found the alabaster eggs. Those are the only two I have in the shop. Not many have gone through my shop over the years. I think you'll find them something really special."

The eggs rolled slightly as Garnet placed them on the countertop next to his other treasures. He quickly reached out to stop them from rolling too much toward the counter's edge. Once they were stilled, Garnet reached for his wallet and gave a slight nod to the shopkeeper. "How much do I owe you for all these treasures?"

Before the shopkeeper could answer Garnet, their attention was shifted to a young boy who at that moment entered through the creaky shop door. He was a scrawny youth with a ruddy complexion. His clothing was ragged and patched, but clean. The boy walked slowly toward the shop counter. The closer he got, the more the sadness in his face became apparent. Once at the counter, he placed both his elbows on the countertop and rested his chin on his crossed arms.

"Jasper," asked the shopkeeper. "what's the matter?"

Jasper's voice was timid and almost squeaky. "Well, I've been thinking. I've been thinking a lot."

"About what?" asked the shopkeeper.

"Books. A book." said Jasper.

"Oh, a book!" exclaimed the shopkeeper.

"Yeh. I'd like a book." Jasper sighed.

The shopkeeper tilted his head to one side. "A book of your own?" He squinted one eye slightly.

"Yes. One of my own. My friends have books. But I don't. We don't have any books in our house." Jasper sighed heavily. "I'd like to have a book of my own to read at home."

The shopkeeper leaned toward Garnet's ear and whispered. "Jasper's family has very little money, and what little they have has to go toward food and heat. Just about everything they have is hand-me-downs. But they're good folks. They try really hard to provide for themselves. Just come up short sometimes."

Garnet looked at the countertop and located *The Wolflings*. As he reached for it, he glanced over at the shopkeeper and winked.

"It just so happens," Garnet said, "that we have just the book for you right here!" Then he handed the book to Jasper.

Jasper gasped. "For me?! Truly, for me?"

"Yes," said Garnet, "for you." He smiled a soft smile at the boy.

Jasper gushed with joy and clasped the book so close to his chest it seemed it would squeeze the breath out of him. Shouting, "Thank you, thank you, thank you!" he dashed out the door.

Garnet looked toward the shopkeeper. "I can always go back to the shelves and find another book that will do nicely for my needs."

The shopkeeper nodded "yes." Then he added, "That boy's family is almost destitute. It is a miracle the boy even knows how to read because he has to do work to help the family get by. You giving that book to Jasper was a very nice thing to do."

"Now, back to what I owe you," started Garnet as he again began to reach for his wallet. But before he could remove it from his pocket, his attention was diverted back to the shop's front door.

"It's Emory," the shopkeeper quietly shared with Garnet.

Emory was an older man, slightly disheveled and looking the worse for wear. He slowly ambled through several shelves near the shop's front area, working his way to the shelves in the music section where Garnet had found the sheet music. With quivering hands, the old man picked up the stack of sheet music and started slowly paging through it. Garnet and the shopkeeper watched Emory with interest and curiosity. Emory held the last sheet in his hand for a moment, then slowly put it down and hung his head. He gave a slight sob, and turned away from the shelf.

The shopkeeper stepped out around from the back of the counter and approached the old man. Gently, the shopkeeper touched Emory's shoulder.

"Emory, what I can help you with?" asked the shopkeeper with a soft kindness in his voice.

Emory turned his head slightly toward the shopkeeper. "I was hoping to find a certain piece I could play on my piano. It's an old piano, but it plays sweetly -- as it always has."

"Well, I have some nice sheets of music here that

would play pretty sweetly on your piano," said the shopkeeper.

The old man sighed, "Yes, they're nice. But they're not the one I was searching for."

"What one was that?" asked the shopkeeper.

"The one that reminds me of the sweet voice of the love of my life," Emory replied. "The one my wife loved so much. She played it for us on our piano the day we were married. That was so many, so many years ago. She passed away a year ago this very day. I wanted to play that music for her today. But it isn't here." Emory gave out a soft sob.

"Emory," said the shopkeeper, "what is the piece?"

"It's no use. It's not here," sighed Emory.

"What is it?" queried Garnet.

"*The Sleeping Beauty Waltz*. We danced to it all night at our wedding." Emory sighed again.

As soon as Garnet heard what Emory said, he took the copy of that very piece of music from his stack on the counter and held it out toward the old man.

"Just so happens that we have a copy of it right here!" said Garnet.

Emory took the music and clutched it close to his breast. Tears welled up in his eyes. The shopkeeper patted Emory on his shoulder and told him to take it home and let it play for him and his wife. Garnet nodded in agreement and smiled a sad smile. Emory shuffled out the shop door and was quickly out of sight.

The shopkeeper placed his hand on Garnet's shoulder. "You are a kind man."

Garnet shrugged. "I still have the other seven pieces in my pile. Those should be sufficient."

The shopkeeper patted Garnet's shoulder a couple more times.

"So, about what I owe you," began Garnet.

But then, the shop door creaked open yet another

time. This time, it was a young girl who had entered the shop. The shopkeeper leaned toward Garnet.

"That's Cordelia. She is always looking for something to give to her younger brother. Rarely finds anything that is just right."

Garnet gave a nod of understanding. He and the shopkeeper watched Cordelia as she wandered through the shop. She would first touch one thing and then another as if her touches would draw out of the objects some special message. She stopped and spent a couple of minutes amongst the toys, and after rummaging through them paused and then turned toward the shop counter. The shopkeeper smiled at Cordelia and asked her if he could help her find anything in particular.

Cordelia answered, "My brother's birthday is tomorrow. I hoped I could find some marbles for him. You know, the glass kind with swirls inside them."

The shopkeeper leaned over to whisper in Garnet's ear. "Cordelia's brother is mostly bedridden. He can only be out of it for a short while. He was born sickly and has never been really well. Never leaves his room. So, if he has any toys, they must be something small he can have in his room."

Garnet's eyes shifted toward Cordelia as his hand moved toward the pouch of marbles he had placed on the counter. He opened the pouch and poured out six marbles, putting them into his pocket. Then, he closed the pouch and handed it to Cordelia.

"Here," Garnet told her, "perhaps these will be okay for your brother?"

Cordelia's eyes widened and she stifled a squeal. "Yes, those would be perfect!"

Garnet gave a sideways glance toward the shopkeeper and continued speaking to her. "Good! Go ahead and put them in your pocket and get them home where they can be of good use."

Cordelia pocketed the marbles, gave a shallow curtsy, and dashed out the shop door.

Garnet looked at the shopkeeper and shrugged his shoulders. "I can get another pouch!"

Then Garnet said, "You won't be making much money today with things going out the door like this!"

The shopkeeper smiled and said, "Maybe not today, but sometime it will come back. Perhaps not as money, but in other important ways."

Garnet then said, "Well, I'd like to pay for each of those things so you are not out the money. I was going to pay for them anyway, so it is no loss for me."

The shopkeeper responded with a smile, "That's okay. I've received my payment already today for those things."

At that moment, a young woman opened the shop door and stepped inside. She paused at the doorway, looked to the left and then to the right, and slowly stepped forward, gently closing the door behind her. For some reason, the door did not squeak as she closed it. She slowly wandered through the shop as the eyes of Garnet and the shopkeeper followed her. She seemed to be searching for something, but wherever she went in the shop she didn't appear to find what she was seeking. The shopkeeper and Garnet whispered quietly to each other about what they thought she was trying to find. Their curiosity was soon answered when the young woman walked to the shop counter.

"Hi," she said timidly. "I was wondering if . . . ."

"If I can help you?" asked the shopkeeper.

The woman gave a soft but shallow smile. She spoke softly, "Yes . . . at least I hope so."

The shopkeeper tilted his head to the side and asked, "What is it, miss . . . miss . . . ."

"Oh!" the woman gasped slightly. "Where are my manners! My name is Ruby. I'm looking for records. Actually, a certain one."

The shopkeeper smiled and asked, "What is its title? Perhaps I have it somewhere in the shop." Ruby responded, "Well, you see, I want to find *The Blue Danube Waltz*." The shopkeeper responded, "Hmmm. *The Blue Danube Waltz*. Why that one?"

Ruby explained, "Well, I've always wanted to be a dancer. But I had to work and could never go to school to learn how to dance. I've had to keep my job as a scullery maid up at the big estate. But I still dance some at home . . . when the shades are closed."

Hard days!" said the shopkeeper.

27

"Yes," Ruby replied. "But you see, my uncle gave me his old gramophone. He cannot hear anymore, so he gave it to me. But I don't have any records to play on it. I haven't had enough money to buy any. I've set aside a few cents each week from my pay, and now I think I have just enough."

"So why *The Blue Danube Waltz*?" asked Garnet.

Ruby answered, "That was one of my uncle's favorites."

The shopkeeper looked puzzled, "But he can't hear it even if you find it, isn't that right?"

Ruby nodded her head and smiled. "No, he can't hear it. But he could see it! I mean, he could see me dancing to it so he could see the music. Maybe he could hear it in his mind."

"I see!" said Garnet. "It just so happens that we have that very record right here on the counter!" He picked up the thick 78 rpm shellac recording and extended it toward Ruby. She leaned forward and looked intently at the record.

"Are you sure you don't want it?" she asked Garnet.

"It was one of several I had in mind, but any of the others will do just fine for me. Here!" Garnet pushed the record closer to Ruby.

She gratefully accepted the record and reached into her small purse.

"No, no! No need for that!" said Garnet. "It's yours. Take it with you and go dance music for your uncle." He smiled.

Ruby gushed thanks after thanks, and gently pressed the record to her chest. As she turned to leave, the shopkeeper patted Garnet on his shoulder and smiled.

After that, Garnet returned to find another book for his nephew. It surprised him to find a second copy of *The Wolflings*. He had certainly not seen it earlier. It was almost magical that another copy just happened to be tucked into the stack of books. Garnet brushed his fingers across its cover and returned to the shop counter with it.

"Well," said the shopkeeper, "this has been a busier day than usual. But a good one!"

Garnet smiled and looked at the counter where he had placed his collection of merchandise. He reached down and picked up the two alabaster eggs. They almost glowed in the light shining through the shop window behind the counter. He smiled as he turned them in his hands. He thought it odd nobody had come into the shop wanting an alabaster egg since it seemed everything else he had selected had been sought by other folks who had come in.

"I guess I'll take these!" Garnet said with a grin. "And what's left of my pile remaining on the countertop . . . and the marbles in my pocket."

The shopkeeper smiled and said, "Nice choices!

That will be six dollars, please." Garnet faked a scowl and shook his head "no." "No, no. Nope. I won't have it! Not at all. That price is all wrong! Besides, there are all these other things, too!"

"Those other things are not for sale," said the shopkeeper.

Garnet was shocked. "What do you mean they're not for sale?!"

"Just what I said," replied the shopkeeper. "I'm giving them to you. All I need is six dollars for the two eggs."

Garnet stammered. "Why would you just give them to me? That's not good business, you know."

The shopkeeper explained. "People are my business. Those things on the countertop, like the ones you gave to those folks who wandered into my shop, are treasures. Treasures are something you give, not sell. A treasure is something given from the heart and helps someone's life be just a little better. Sometimes, treasures are big things, and sometimes they're small things. All that stuff that you gave away today were small things to you and me, but were very big to those folks who received them. You had every intention of paying for them, so you had it in your heart to give something to others that were treasures to them. And you, my friend, are a big treasure."

Garnet had a brief thought about how hard and long he had worked for the money he clasped in his hand. Then, after a soft sigh, he grinned and handed the shopkeeper his $50. "This," said Garnet, "is the better price for these eggs!" The shopkeeper stammered, but

Garnet put up his hand to shush him.

Garnet explained, "What you have in your shop is far more valuable than anything you have on the shelves. I will remember what I've been given here today, in your shop, from you. It will be something I will always remember, and keep it in my heart as a real treasure. I want you to have this so you can continue giving as you do to those folks who come in here seeking something . . . something they are not likely to find in most places . . . and leaving with more than they sought. I will be leaving with far more than what I sought, I can assure you! I am much richer now than when I walked through your shop's door!"

With that, Garnet picked up the two alabaster eggs, wrapped them in his kerchief, and gently pushed them into his coat pocket. As he reached for the gramophone, the shopkeeper picked it up first and said, "Here, let me get this for you! It's time to close the shop and I need a walk. Let me help you get this home." He smiled.

Garnet then took up the book, the sheet music, and records, and the two walked to the door. They stepped outside, and the shopkeeper turned to close and lock the shop door. Afterward, they both turned together toward the street and briskly walked down it as they continued to live life well.

End Notes

The Music:

The Emperor's Waltz by Johann Strauss, Jr

The Blue Danube Waltz by Johann Strauss, Jr.

The Water Music by George Frideric Handel

Royal Fireworks by George Frideric Handel

A Little Night Music by Amadeus Mozart

Serenade for Strings by Pyotr IlyichTchaikovsky

The Sleeping Beauty Waltz by Pyotr Ilyich Tchaikovsky

Canon in D by Johann Pachelbel

The Treasure Gems:

Garnet -- A Middle-English name derived from the word "gernet", meaning the dark red color of pomegranate that garnet crystals resemble.

Jasper -- A Persian name derived from the Latin name Gaspar, meaning "bringer of treasure"

Emory -- Old English surname derived from the Germanic name "Emmerich", meaning "strength"

Cordelia -- Anglicized version of Creiddylad in Welsh, meaning "jewel of the sea"

Ruby -- Alternative spelling of the Rubi in Spanish meaning a gemstone of deep red color

Alabaster:

Ancient alabaster is a form of the mineral calcite (calcium carbonate) found in the Middle East, including Egypt and Mesopotamia. It is easy to carve with a knife and dye. Some of the most finely carved and dyed alabaster originates in Italy.

www.ingramcontent.com/pod-product-compliance
Lightning Source LLC
LaVergne TN
LVHW070939070526
838199LV00035B/657